Tallyho, Pinkerton!

STORY AND PICTURES BY

Steven Kellogg

A Puffin Pied Piper

Dial Books for Young Readers
375 Hudson Street
New York, New York 10014

Library of Congress Catalog Card Number: 82-2341
First Pied Piper Printing 1985
Printed in the United States of America
COBE

7 9 10 8
A Pied Piper Book is a registered trademark of
Dial Books for Young Readers,
a division of Penguin Books USA Inc.
® TM 1,163,686 and ® TM 1,054,312.

TALLYHO, PINKERTON!
is published in a hardcover edition by
Dial Books for Young Readers.
ISBN 0-14-054710-X

The process art consists of black line-drawings, black halftones,
and full-color washes. The black line is prepared and
photographed separately for greater contrast and sharpness.
The full-color washes and the black halftones are
prepared with ink, crayons, and paints on the reverse side
of the black line-drawing. They are then camera-separated and
reproduced as red, blue, yellow, and black halftones.

Today in school we studied birds and mammals.
Did you know that Pinkerton and Rose are both mammals?

For homework we're supposed to go on a field trip and identify
ten different birds and mammals. I'll start right here, and
then I'll go to the woods.

Since wild birds and mammals are shy and hard to find,
I'll take Pinkerton and Rose along to help me.

Wait! It's a perfect afternoon for a walk in the woods.
I'll pack a picnic and come too.

Look! My helpers have already spotted the first bird: a scarlet tanager!

Pinkerton! Rose! Come back! We want to identify
the birds, not chase them!

Hurry! I think they went this way!

We'll land here. These woods are filled with foxes.

Stake the balloon and post the signs. Our classes will begin in the next clearing.

Rose! Pinkerton! Where are you?

SILENCE! You are disrupting my class!

Excuse us, but our cat and dog were helping me with my homework, and now they're lost in the woods. Have you seen them?

LESSON TWO
Learn to recognize
THE GRAY FOX

LESSON ONE
Learn to recognize
THE RED FOX

We can't be bothered with stray animals. We're looking for the noble red fox.

I'd like to see a red fox. He'd be number four on my list. Maybe we could all search together.

Certainly not! This is a private hunting class. You'll have to leave.

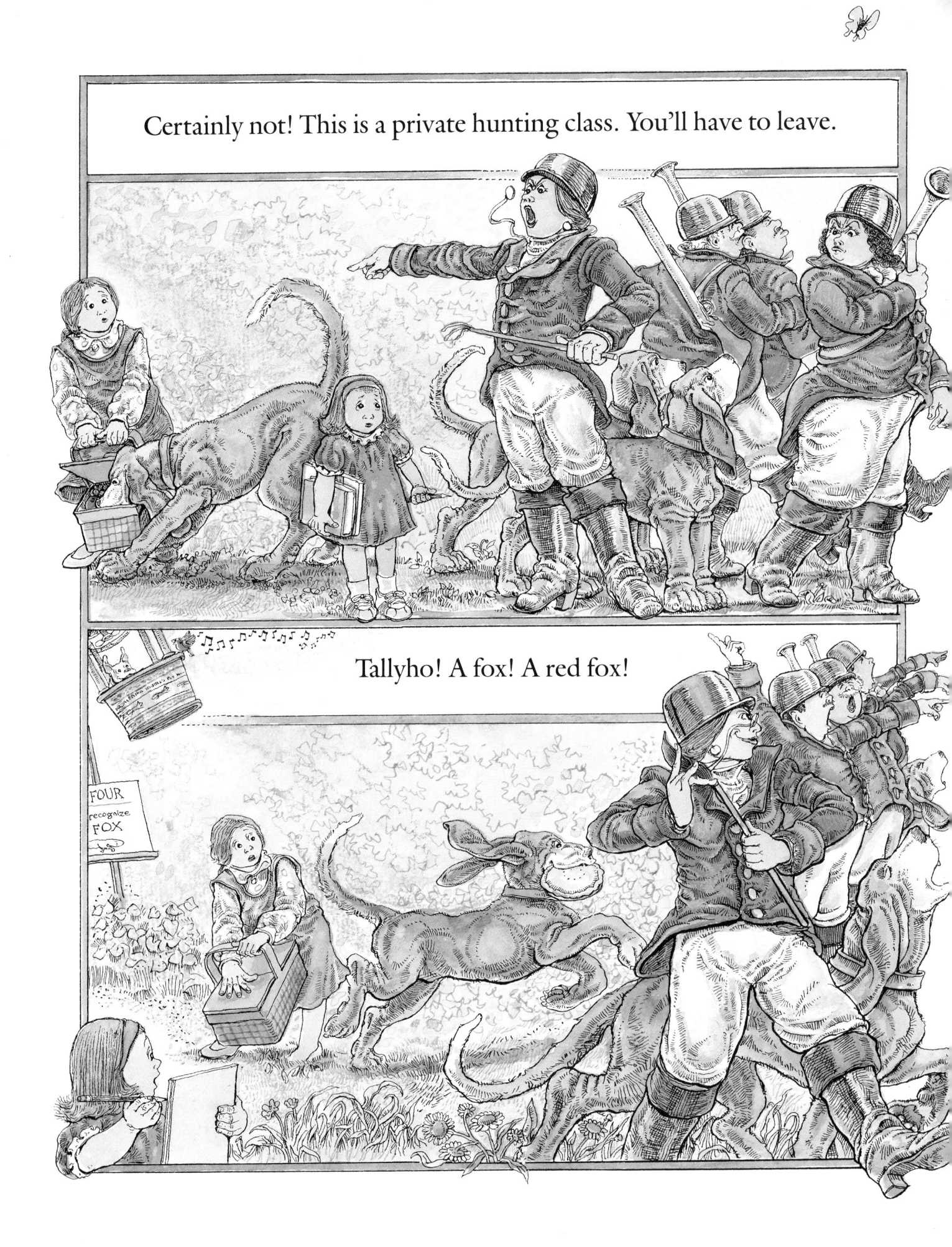

Tallyho! A fox! A red fox!

DR. ALEASHA KIBBLE'S FOX HUNTING ACADEMY

Stop shooting, you blockheads, and leash your hounds at once!

I said, STOP SHOOTING!

IDIOTS! This is not a fox! Remember Lesson One!

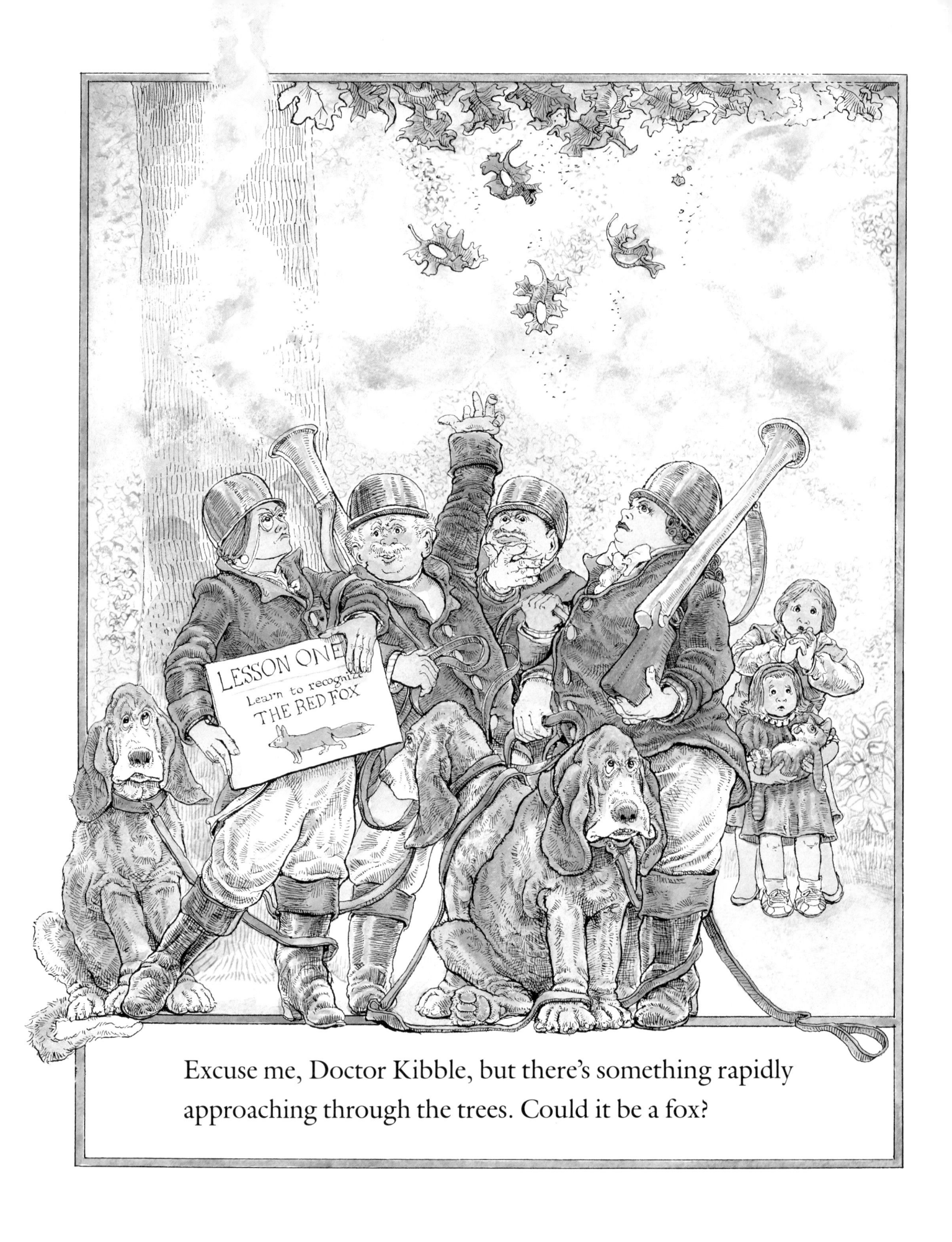

Excuse me, Doctor Kibble, but there's something rapidly
approaching through the trees. Could it be a fox?

It's an invasion from outer space. Run for your lives!

It's Pinkerton!

Class, let us leave these fools and return to the hunt.

Never mind them. We'll find a good spot for our picnic, and then I'll finish my homework.

LESSON ONE
Learn to recognize
THE RED FOX

I'm glad that Pinkerton made friends with the scarlet tanager.

PINKERTON

Tallyho! We're hot on the trail!

Well done, class. You have cornered a very rare striped fox.

Excuse me, but he isn't a striped fox.
And I think you'd better not bother him.

Ignore her, class, and surround that fox before it escapes!

Well, this has turned out to be a crazy afternoon walk in the woods. It'll be dark soon, and by the time we clean up the picnic, I'm afraid you won't be able to finish that homework list.

TEN BIRDS AND
MAMMALS I
HAVE SEEN:
1. Rose, A cat.
2. Pinkerton,
A Great
Dane.
3. The Scarlet
Tanager.
4. A Striped Skunk.
5.
6.
7.
8.
9.
10.